# Weird Plants

Tamara Einstein &
Einstein Sisters

KidsWorld

# Contents

What are Plants? ..........................................4

Fungi ...........................................................4

Lichens .......................................................5

Eating for a Living .....................................6

Venus Flytrap ............................................7

Pitcher Plant .............................................8

Sundew .....................................................10

Strangler Fig ............................................12

Biggest and Smallest ..............................14

Biggest Living Organism.........................16

Largest Flowers ......................................18

Rafflesia ..................................................18

Titan Arum...............................................20

Talipot Palm ............................................21

Queen Victoria Water Lily ......................22

Living Stones ..........................................24

Bullhorn Acacia .......................................... 26

Squirting Cucumber ................................... 28

Baobab Tree ............................................... 30

Passionflower ............................................. 32

Flying Duck Orchid ..................................... 34

Darwin's Slipper Orchid ............................. 36

Hot Lips ...................................................... 38

Dragon Fruit ............................................... 40

Chinese Lantern ......................................... 42

Mimosa ....................................................... 44

Sloth Algae ................................................. 46

Fairy Puke ................................................... 48

Pixie Cup .................................................... 50

Basket Stinkhorn ........................................ 52

Bleeding Tooth ........................................... 54

Veiled Lady ................................................. 56

Anemone Stinkhorn .................................... 58

Bird's Nest Fungus ..................................... 60

Foxfire ........................................................ 62

# What are Plants?

Plants are living organisms that live everywhere in the world. Most plants are green and can turn sunlight into energy to grow and make seeds or fruit. Some plants cannot do this, and have other ways of making energy.

Fungi or mushrooms, were once thought to be plants, but we now know that fungi are not true plants. They cannot make energy from sunlight.

# Fungi

Some plants, such as grass and trees, are familiar to us. Even the vegetables and fruit in the supermarket come from plants. In this book are plants that are much less familar and very weird!

Lichens are a special kind of organism. They are a combination of a fungus with an algae (a kind of tiny plant).

# Lichens

5

# Eating for a Living

The **Venus flytrap** is probably the most famous plant that is capable of fast movement. Not only can it move, but it catches bugs to eat!

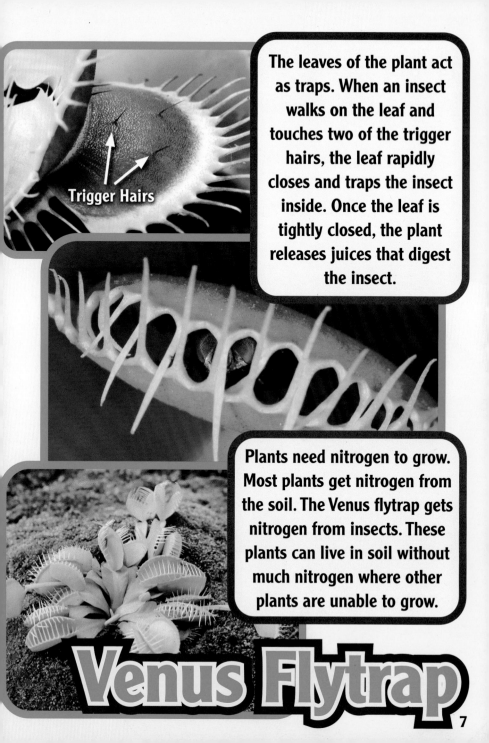

**Trigger Hairs**

The leaves of the plant act as traps. When an insect walks on the leaf and touches two of the trigger hairs, the leaf rapidly closes and traps the insect inside. Once the leaf is tightly closed, the plant releases juices that digest the insect.

Plants need nitrogen to grow. Most plants get nitrogen from the soil. The Venus flytrap gets nitrogen from insects. These plants can live in soil without much nitrogen where other plants are unable to grow.

# Venus Flytrap

# Pitcher Plant

The pitcher plant
is another kind of
carnivorous (meat-eating)
plant. It also eats insects.
These odd-looking plants
grow in forests or
mashland areas.

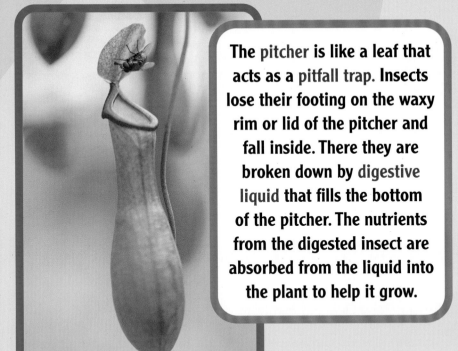

The pitcher is like a leaf that acts as a pitfall trap. Insects lose their footing on the waxy rim or lid of the pitcher and fall inside. There they are broken down by digestive liquid that fills the bottom of the pitcher. The nutrients from the digested insect are absorbed from the liquid into the plant to help it grow.

Pitcher plants make pitchers to eat insects, but the plants also make flowers. The pitchers are the reddish leaves that grow close to the ground, and the pinkish flowers grow at the tops of tall stems.

9

# Sundew

The sundew plant is another carnivorous plant that attracts insects using drops sweet of liquid on its leaves.

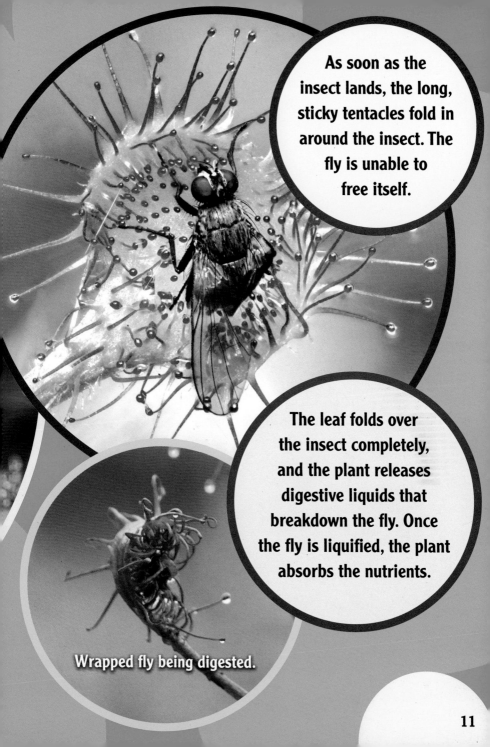

As soon as the insect lands, the long, sticky tentacles fold in around the insect. The fly is unable to free itself.

The leaf folds over the insect completely, and the plant releases digestive liquids that breakdown the fly. Once the fly is liquified, the plant absorbs the nutrients.

Wrapped fly being digested.

11

Some tropical forests are so thick with trees that sunlight never reaches the ground. Young trees cannot grow without sunlight. The strangler fig has a unique solution to the problem. It relies on birds to drop its seeds in the tops of other trees. The fig then grows roots down the main trunk of the host tree to get to the soil.

# Strangler Fig

As the strangler fig grows, it can almost completely surround the host tree trunk with its roots. The strangler fig does not kill the host tree.

Sometimes, the host tree becomes stronger and more able to survive storms because of the thickened trunk. Even if the inner host tree dies, the strangler fig will still survive. Without the host tree, the trunk of the strangler fig looks like hollow mesh.

# Biggest and Smallest

The smallest plant in the world is called spotless watermeal. Each little green dot is a single plant!

The largest leaves in the world grow on the raffia palm. Each leaf looks like a branch and can be more than 80 feet (25 meters) long!

The largest trees in the world are the redwood trees. The largest tree in the world (shown here) even has a name! It is called General Sherman after a famous American military man.

Another redwood, called Hyperion, is the tallest tree in the world. It is 380 feet (116 meters) tall. That's as tall as some city buildings!

# Biggest Living Organism

The biggest living organism in the world is an aspen clone. An aspen tree grows new trees by sending out sprouts from its roots. That means that a clump of aspen trees is actually the same plant, called a clone. Even though a clone looks like a bunch of separate trees, they are all the same plant because they share the same roots.

The largest aspen clone is named Pando. Pando is believed to weigh more than 13 million pounds (6 million kilograms), that's more than the weight of the water in two Olympic-sized swimming pools! Pando is also the oldest living organism at about 80,000 years old!

Aspen clones are easy to see in the autumn. All of the trees that are part of the same clone turn yellow at the same time!

# Largest Flowers

The rafflesia is one of the weirdest plants of all. It has no stem, no true roots and no leaves. The rafflesia doesn't even grow in the ground. It has thin root-like structures that grow inside a host plant.

# Rafflesia

The only part of this plant you can see is the large flower. It is the largest single flower in the world. The flower petals can be almost 4 feet (1.2 meters) across!

Rafflesia flowers smell like rotting meat. The horrible smell attracts insects. The insects pollinate the flowers as they fly from flower to flower.

# Titan Arum

The titan arum has the largest unbranched inflorescence of any plant. An inflorescence is a plant structure that supports many smaller flowers.

Although it looks like a flower, this titan arum inflorescence has hundreds of tiny flowers inside the base. The largest titan arum inflorescence was more than 10 feet (3 meters) tall!

# Talipot Palm

The talipot palm has the largest branched inflorescence in the world. The puffy yellow branches at the top of each palm tree shown here are each a single-branched inflorescence with millions of flowers!

# Queen Victoria Water Lily

The amazing Queen Victoria water lily grows large, round leaves or pads that float on the water. These leaves can be up to 10 feet (3 meters) across. That's bigger than a dining room table!

The underside of the lily pad has large veins and ribs that help support its weight and allow it to float. A small child could even sit atop a large lily pad!

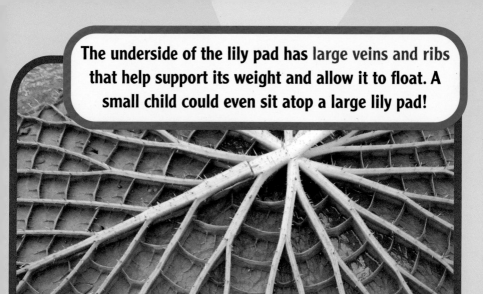

Many birds and other animals walk on top of the water lilies, looking for bugs and other small critters to eat.

# Living Stones

Living stones are also called pebble plants because they look like stones, and they grow among stones. Each plant is just two leaves growing side by side. The leaves are succulent, meaning they are thick and fleshy, holding lots of water.

Living stones make a single flower that sprouts from between the two leaves.

Living stones are found mostly in southern Africa. They have colors similar to the colors of the stones where they grow. This camouflage protects them from being eaten. How many living stones can you count on this page?

# Bullhorn Acacia

Each bullhorn acacia has a special relationship with a colony of acacia ants. An ant colony starts with a single queen. She chews a hole in a thorn of the plant and lays eggs inside it. The eggs hatch, and the colony grows.

Hole Made by Ants

As the colony grows, the ants make holes in more and more of the thorns on the tree. A large colony in a single tree can have several thousand ants!

Beltian Bodies

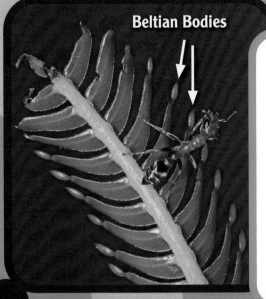

The ants protect the tree they live on by killing other insects and biting animals that may eat the leaves. In return, the tree feeds the ants with Beltian bodies. These are little packets of food that form at the tips of the leaves.

# Squirting Cucumber

The **squirting cucumber** is a mildly poisonous plant that has pretty yellow flowers and pickle-sized fruits. The fruits hang from long stems and are covered with spines. The fruits are filled with liquid and seeds that come under increasing pressure as the fruit ripens.

When something brushes against the spines of a ripe cucumber, it separates from the stem. The liquid is under such high pressure that it shoots out the hole, sending the seeds up to 20 feet (6 meters) away and propelling the cucumber to the ground.

# Baobab Tree

Of the six species of baobab trees in the world, the largest is Grandidier's baobab, which is native to Madagascar. This tree is sometimes called the upside-down tree because the top branches look like roots. This amazing tree is an endangered species.

The flowers of the baobab tree open at dusk. They open so fast you can even see the movement!

# Passionflower

Passionflowers are beautiful vines found in North and South America. There are about 550 different species! Each species produces different flowers, but all are delicate and amazing.

The showy flowers are pollinated by bees, bats and hummingbirds. The sword-billed hummingbird is a specialist pollinator for 37 kinds of passionflowers!

Sword-billed hummingbird

The fruit, called passionfruit, is about the size of a plum. When the fruit is ripe is looks black and lumpy. The inside has many seeds in jelly-like sacs. They are delicious!

# Flying Duck Orchid

As its name suggests, this orchid grows a flower that looks like a flying duck! The remarkable **flying duck orchid** is found only in Australia.

The delicate flowers attract insects, like sawflies, that pollinate the flower. Although people have tried to grow this orchid in pots, it never does well. It is best left to grow and flower in the wild.

# Darwin's Slipper Orchid

Looking like little aliens carrying baskets, this flower, called the Darwin's slipper orchid, can be found in the mountains of Tierra del Fuego, the southernmost tip of South America.

These orchids are named after Charles Darwin, a famous scientist. More than 150 years ago, Darwin visited Tierra del Fuego, and his observations of plants and animals in South America gave him the ideas about evolution.

# Hot Lips

Looking like lips with red lipstick ready for a kiss, hot lips is an understory plant (one that grows on the forest floor and needs little light to grow). This plant lives in the rainforests of Central and South America. It has many medicinal uses but has become endangered by over-harvesting.

The bright red lips of this plant are not actually the flower. They are showy bracts (special leaves) that attract butterflies and hummingbirds to their unscented flowers. The plant relies on butterflies and hummingbirds for pollination.

# Dragon Fruit

The **dragon fruit** gets its name from its thick, leathery skin. This red skin has the appearance of large scales, much like the skin of a dragon. Dragon fruits are delicious!

The dragon fruit is native to North and South America, but it is now grown around the world for its tasty fruit.

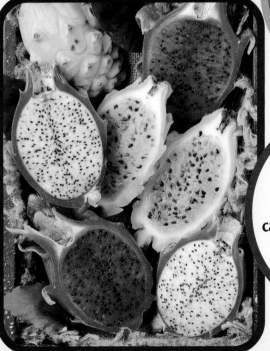

The fleshy fruit can be pink or white, and the leathery skin can be yellow or pink. The flesh tastes a bit like watermelon!

# Chinese Lantern

The Chinese lantern has fruits that are covered in bright red, papery leaves. It grows in Europe and Asia. The ripe fruits are used in many medicinal remedies.

The fruit starts out small and green, and as it ripens, it turns yellow then red. The ripe red paper around the fruit resembles a traditional Chinese lantern. As the fruit ages, the paper disintegrates, leaving the ripe fruit inside a delicate, lacey pouch.

# Mimosa

The mimosa is one of only a few plants that has rapid movement. It grows around the world, but it is only native to Central and South America.

Another name for the plant is touch-me-not. When something touches a leaf, the leaflets quickly fold up. The leaflets also fold up in response to blowing or shaking.

The movement is believed to scare away insects that land on the plant, hoping to eat it or lay eggs on it.

Sloths are animals that live in trees in the rainforests of Central and South America. They are famous for being extremely slow moving. People joke that they move so slowly that algae grows on them!

# Sloth Algae

The algae that grows in the fur of sloths is actually found nowhere else! The green color camouflages the sloths in the trees. The algae also attracts a fungus, and both help to protect the sloth from parasites. Finally, when the sloth grooms itself, it eats some of the algae, providing the animal with essential nutrients!

# Fairy Puke

If you walk in the forests of North America, you might encounter this crusty green lichen with pink spots. It often looks like it is splattered over a rock or mossy log. Its appearance is why it is lovingly named fairy puke.

The green part of this lichen gets its color from a kind of algae. The pink blobs are the reproductive part of the fungus. They are like tiny mushrooms.

# Pixie Cup

The pixie cup lichen gets its name from the cup-like structure that it forms. These cups are no bigger than one inch (2.5 cm) high.

Like tiny goblets, the pixie cups stand upright. Unlike a real cup or goblet, they are not meant to hold liquid.

The cups are covered in a greenish powder. A microscope is needed to see that each grain of powder is a package containing a few algal cells and a few fungal cells so the lichen can reproduce.

# Basket Stinkhorn

The most striking feature of this unusual mushroom is that it is hollow with interlacing branches. And like the name says, it also stinks!

The basket stinkhorn emerges from the soil in a round, egg-like sac. It then breaks through the sac and expands into the shape of a basket. The inside of each branch is covered in goo that smells like rotting meat.

The smell attracts flies that get spores on them. The flies then carry the spores to new locations, so that new basket stinkhorns can grow.

# Bleeding Tooth

The unusual bleeding tooth fungus gets its name from the tooth-like structure on its underside and the blood-like drops that cover the top surface.

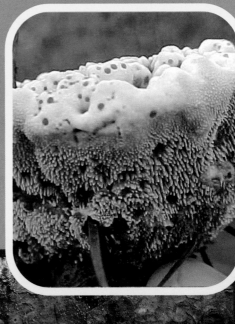

Like other mushrooms, this fungus has a large network of roots (hyphae) that grow around the roots of conifer trees. The tree roots and the hyphae exchange nutrients. The tree makes nutrients that the fungus needs, and the fungus makes nutrients that the tree needs. Relationships like this that benefit both organisms is called symbiosis. A good trade!

# Veiled Lady

The veiled lady mushroom grows at a speed of about 1/5 inch (5 mm) a minute! This makes it one of the fastest growing organisms on the planet. If you're patient, you can even watch it grow!

Veiled lady mushrooms grow in tropical forests around the world. Like other stinkhorn mushrooms, this one has a terrible odor. Nevertheless, it is thought to be a delicacy and often eaten in soup!

# Anemone Stinkhorn

Looking like a strange alien, the anemone stinkhorn is commonly found in Australia. It can grow to about the size of a mango.

When the stinkhorn fungus produces a fruiting body (mushroom), an egg-shaped case first emerges from the soil. Next, the mature stinkhorn emerges from the "egg."

This mushroom gets its name from the brown goo in its center. The goo smells like rotting meat. The smell attracts flies that will spread its spores.

# Bird's Nest Fungus

The unusual bird's nest fungus can be found throughout much of the world. The fruiting body (mushroom) resembles a tiny bird's nest with eggs inside!

The nest functions as a splash cup. When raindrops land in the cup the "eggs" are splashed out. They sometimes land as far as a meter (3 feet) away! The "eggs" contain the spores that grow into more fungi.

Bird's nest fungi can be found in small groups or large clusters. They grow on rotting wood.

# Foxfire

At night, some mushrooms glow bright green! **Foxfire** is not the name of any one mushroom. It refers to the ability to glow in the dark. It is also sometimes called fairy fire.

No one really knows why certain mushrooms glow. Maybe the light attracts insects to spread spores, or maybe the light startles hungry animals and protects the mushroom from being eaten.

More than 80 different kinds of mushrooms can produce foxfire!

The Publisher: KidsWorld Books

**Library and Archives Canada Cataloguing in Publication**

Title: Weird plants / Tamara Einstein & Einstein Sisters.

Names: Einstein, Tamara, author. | Einstein Sisters, author.

Identifiers: Canadiana (print) 202003732502 | Canadiana (ebook) 20200373269 | ISBN 9781988183589 (softcover) | ISBN 9781988183596 (EPUB)

Subjects: LCSH: Plants—Juvenile literature.

Classification: LCC QK49 .E36 2021 | DDC j580—dc23

*Front cover:* Sundew by Argument, Getty Images.

*Back cover:* Darwin's slipper orchids by MarcelStrelow, Getty Images; Venus flytrap by CathyKeifer, Getty Images; Living stones by Lithopsian, Wikimedia Commons.

*Photo credits:* From Wikimedia Commons: Amada44 49 ; Angelos Papadimitriou 53a ; Bernard Spragg 51ab ; Bernypisa 54b ; Cephas 9b ; Christian Fischer 14a ; Daniel B. Wheeler 54a ; Darvin DeShazer 55 ; David Gough (Spacepleb) 52 ; Dick Culbert 39b ; Franz Xaver 39a ; Gerardolagunes 53b ; Hyunjung Kim 57a ; Jason Hollinger 5b ; Len Worthington 59ab ; Lithopsian 24b ; Luru Ly 31b ; OhWeh 48b ; Rasbak 43c ; Ryan Somma 26a ; Suguri F 23a ; Tigerente 48a ; When on Earth 38. From Getty Images: Alberto Carrera 46; Alex Frood 63a; aLittleSilhouetto 7a, 44; amedved 20; Argument 10; BING-JHEN HONG 41a; Bob Balestri 33a; Brunomartinsimagens 21; CathyKeifer 6; Chaiwat Trisongkram 43b; Chansom Pantip 2, 3; Citysqwirl 33b; ClaireLucia 43a; Connie Kerr 13b, 56; Court Whelan 30-31; CreativeNature_nl 11b; Daniel Lange 47a; Denny35463 16-17; Geoview 47b; GerhardSaueracker 37; goodgold99 7c; grafxart8888 4b; guliver-max 51b; HarryHuber 42; hekakoskinen 11a, 50, 60b; Jamo5 62; JokoHarismoyo 45a; KarenHBlack 12; kellymarken 9a; Ken Griffiths 34, 35; Kesu01 33d; Kovaleva_Ka 40a; lucky-photographer 15; macca236 63b; MarcelStrelow 36; marcouliana 7b; mazzzur 19; mongkol konkamol 45b; mspoli 13a; Nataliia Mysak 41b; quickshooting 4-5; RAVINDRAN JOHN SMITH 18; sagarmanis 8; SangSanit 40b; SaskiaAcht 28; sebastianosecondi 32; shakzu 27a; slpu9945 33c; Svetlana Chekhlova 23b; Teen00000 57b; Venus Kaewyoo 24a; wika1979 22. From Flickr: Coconino National Forest, Ariz. 17b ; Erik Burton 61 ; Feroze Omardeen 26b ; Jason Hollinger 61a ; Judy Gallagher 27b ; Michael Whitehead 60a. From Youtube: MPBirds 29.

We acknowledge the financial support of the Government of Canada.
Nous reconnaissons l'appui financier du gouvernement du Canada.

Funded by the Government of Canada
Financé par le gouvernement du Canada | **Canadä**

*PC:* 38-1